SAM WHO??

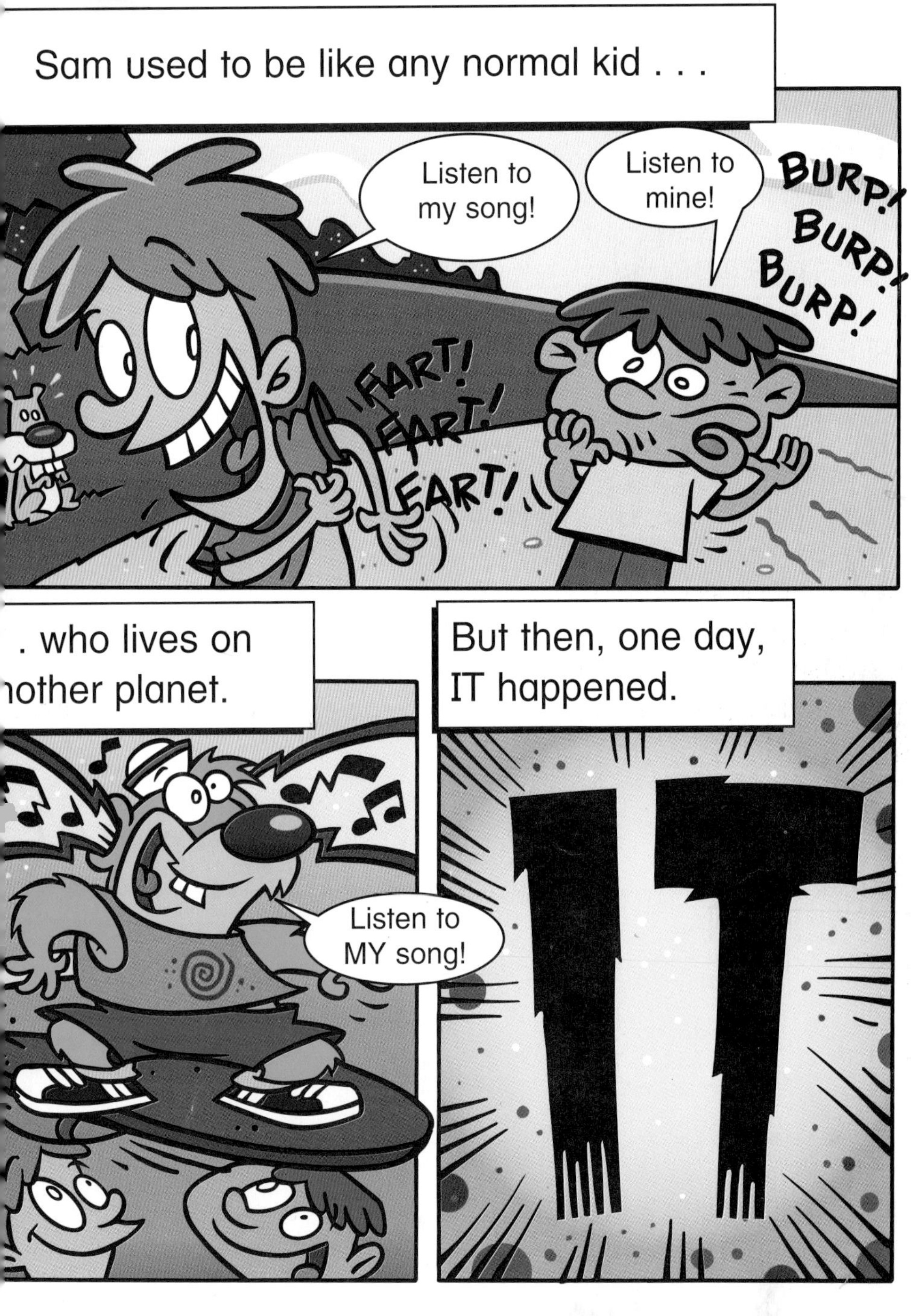
Sam used to be like any normal kid . . .
Listen to my song!
Listen to mine!
BURP! BURP! BURP!
FART! FART! FART!
. who lives on
nother planet.
Listen to MY song!
But then, one day, IT happened.
IT

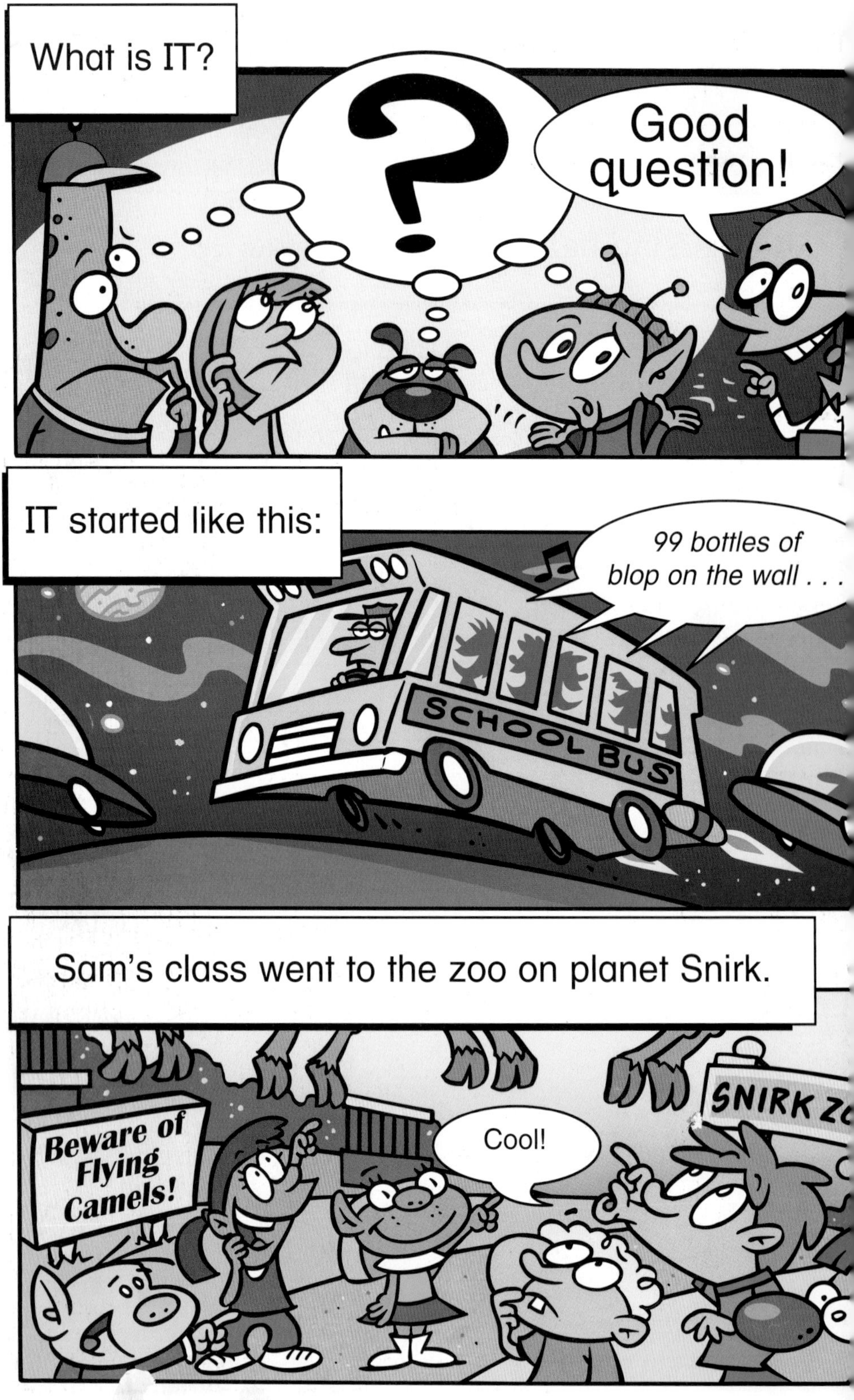
What is IT?
Good question!
IT started like this:
99 bottles of blop on the wall . . .
SCHOOL BUS
Sam's class went to the zoo on planet Snirk.
Beware of Flying Camels!
Cool!

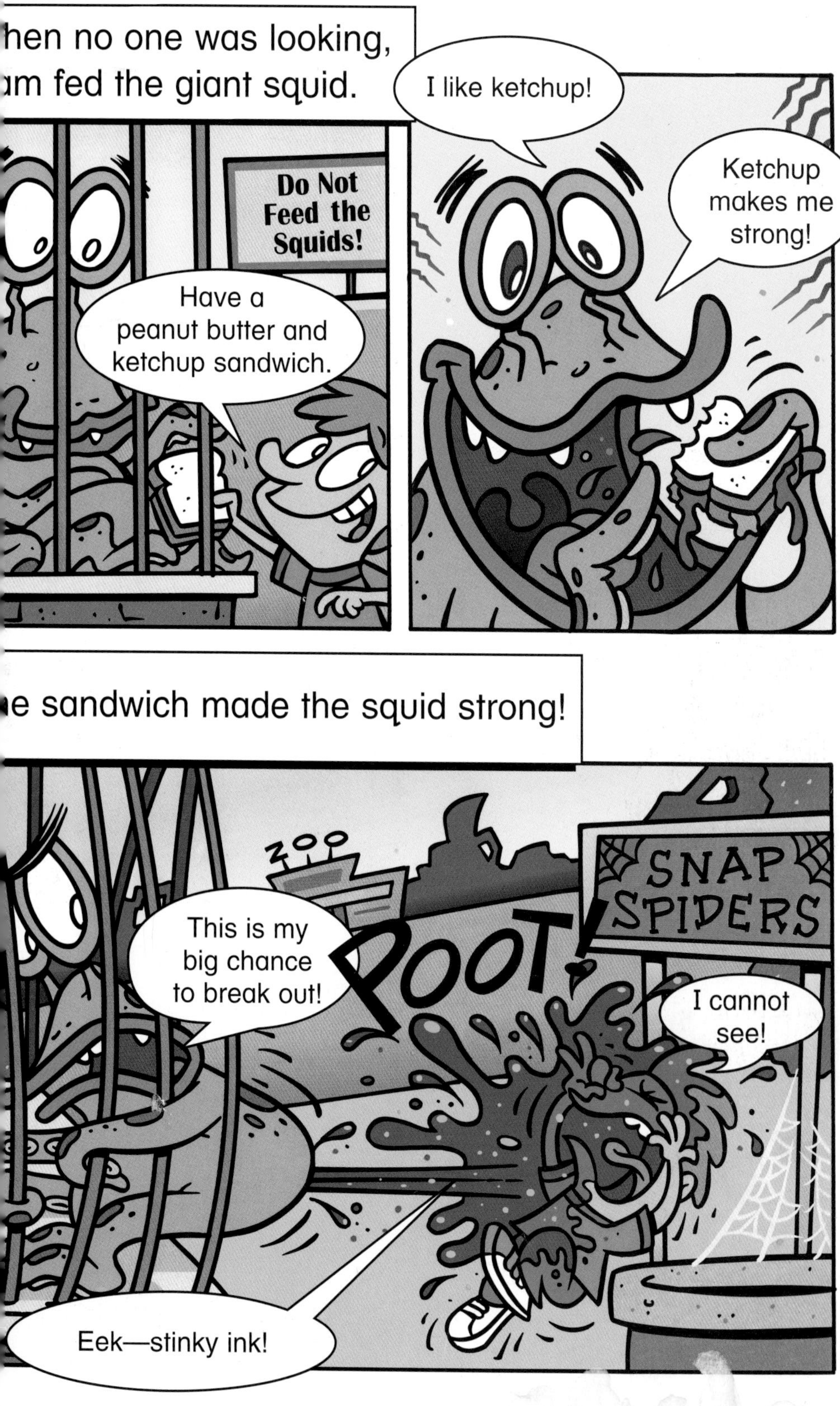
hen no one was looking,
am fed the giant squid.
Do Not Feed the Squids!
Have a peanut butter and ketchup sandwich.
I like ketchup!
Ketchup makes me strong!
e sandwich made the squid strong!
ZOO
SNAP SPIDERS
This is my big chance to break out!
POOT!
I cannot see!
Eek—stinky ink!

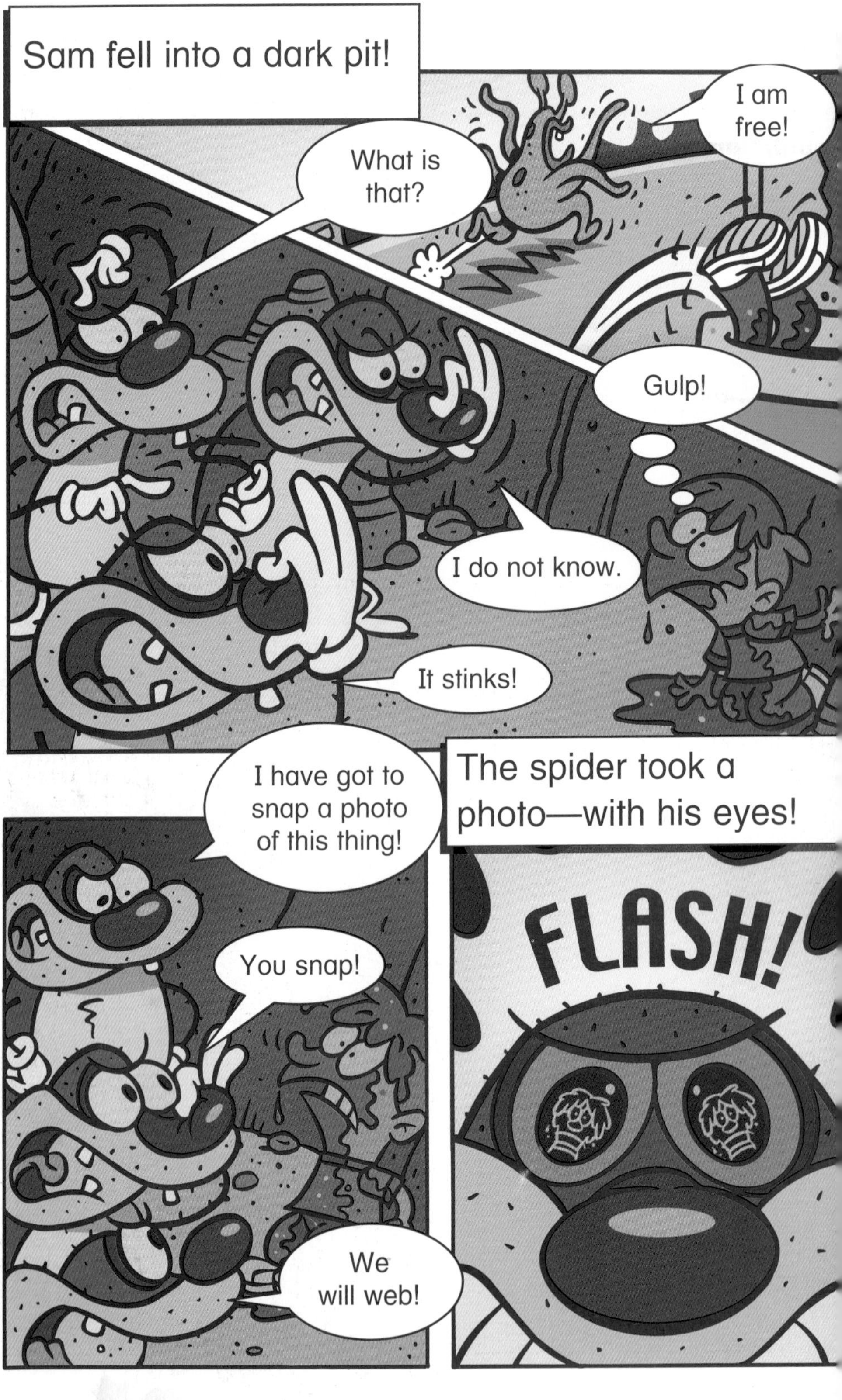

Sam fell into a dark pit!
I am free!
What is that?
Gulp!
I do not know.
It stinks!
The spider took a photo—with his eyes!
I have got to snap a photo of this thing!
You snap!
We will web!
FLASH!

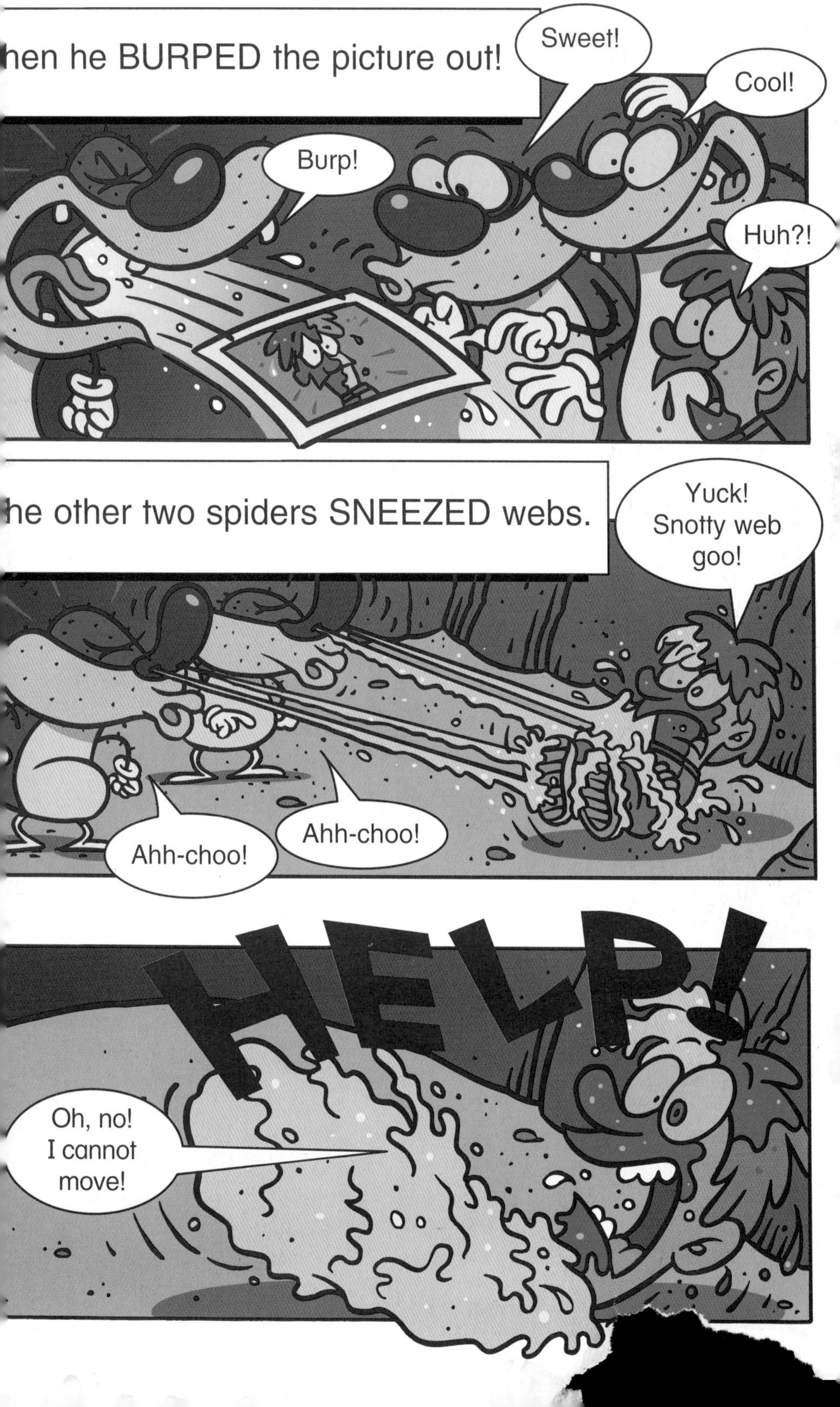
hen he BURPED the picture out!
Sweet!
Cool!
Burp!
Huh?!
he other two spiders SNEEZED webs.
Yuck! Snotty web goo!
Ahh-choo!
Ahh-choo!
HELP!
Oh, no! I cannot move!

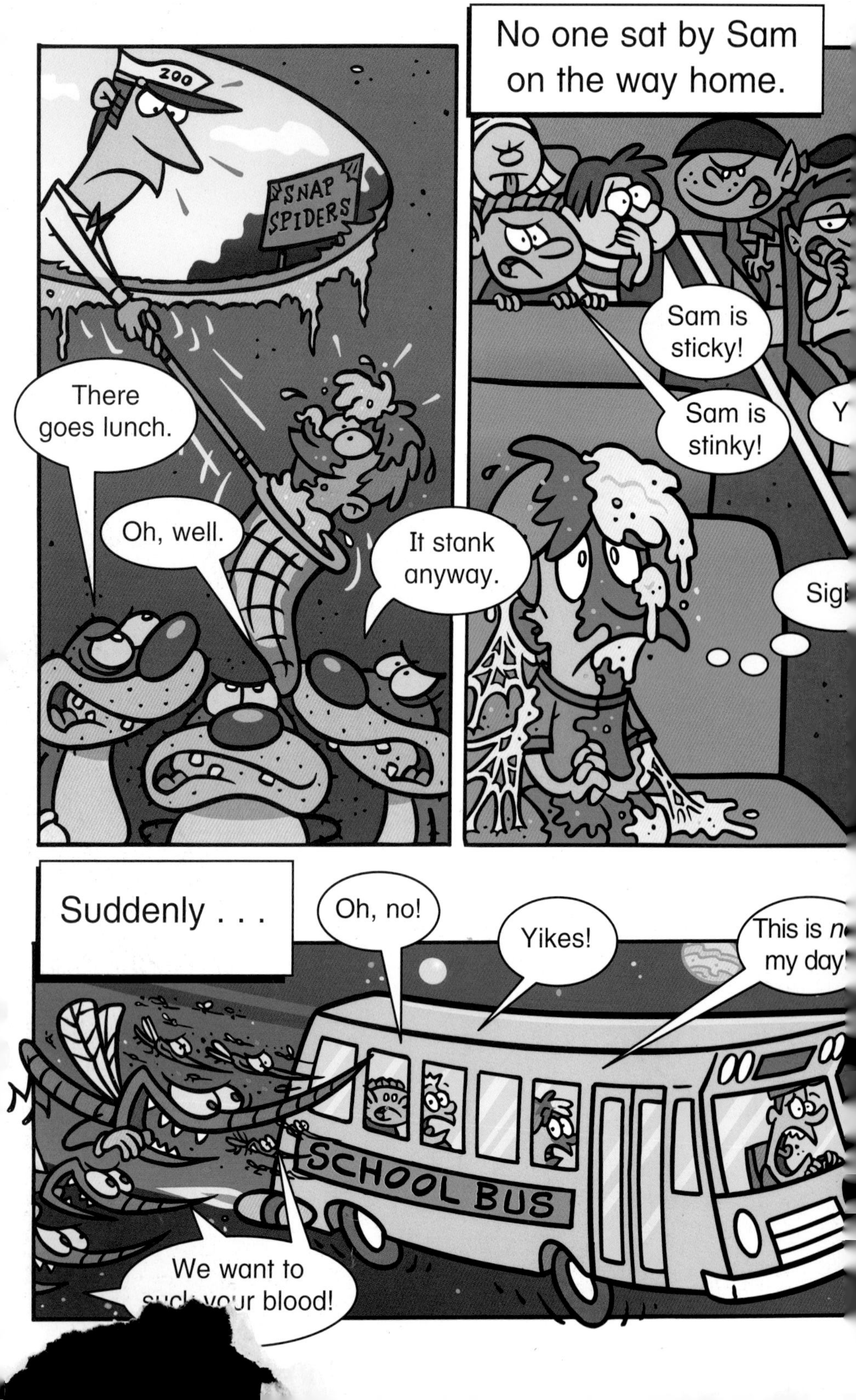
200
SNAP SPIDERS
There goes lunch.
Oh, well.
It stank anyway.
No one sat by Sam on the way home.
Sam is sticky!
Sam is stinky!
Suddenly . . .
Oh, no!
Yikes!
SCHOOL BUS
We want to suck your blood!

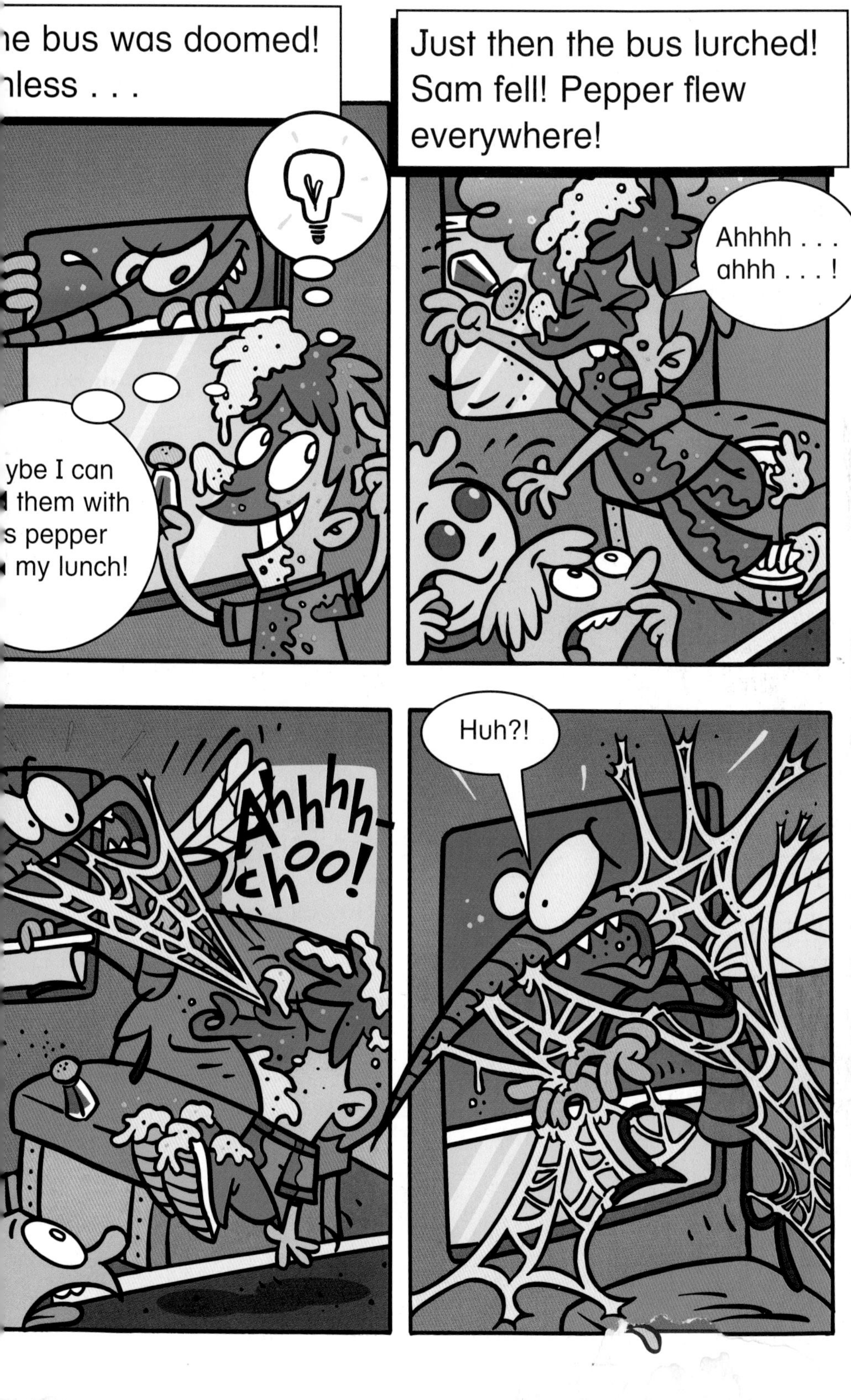
e bus was doomed!
less . . .
ybe I can them with s pepper my lunch!
Just then the bus lurched! Sam fell! Pepper flew everywhere!
Ahhhh . . . ahhh . . . !
Ahhhh-choo!
Huh?!

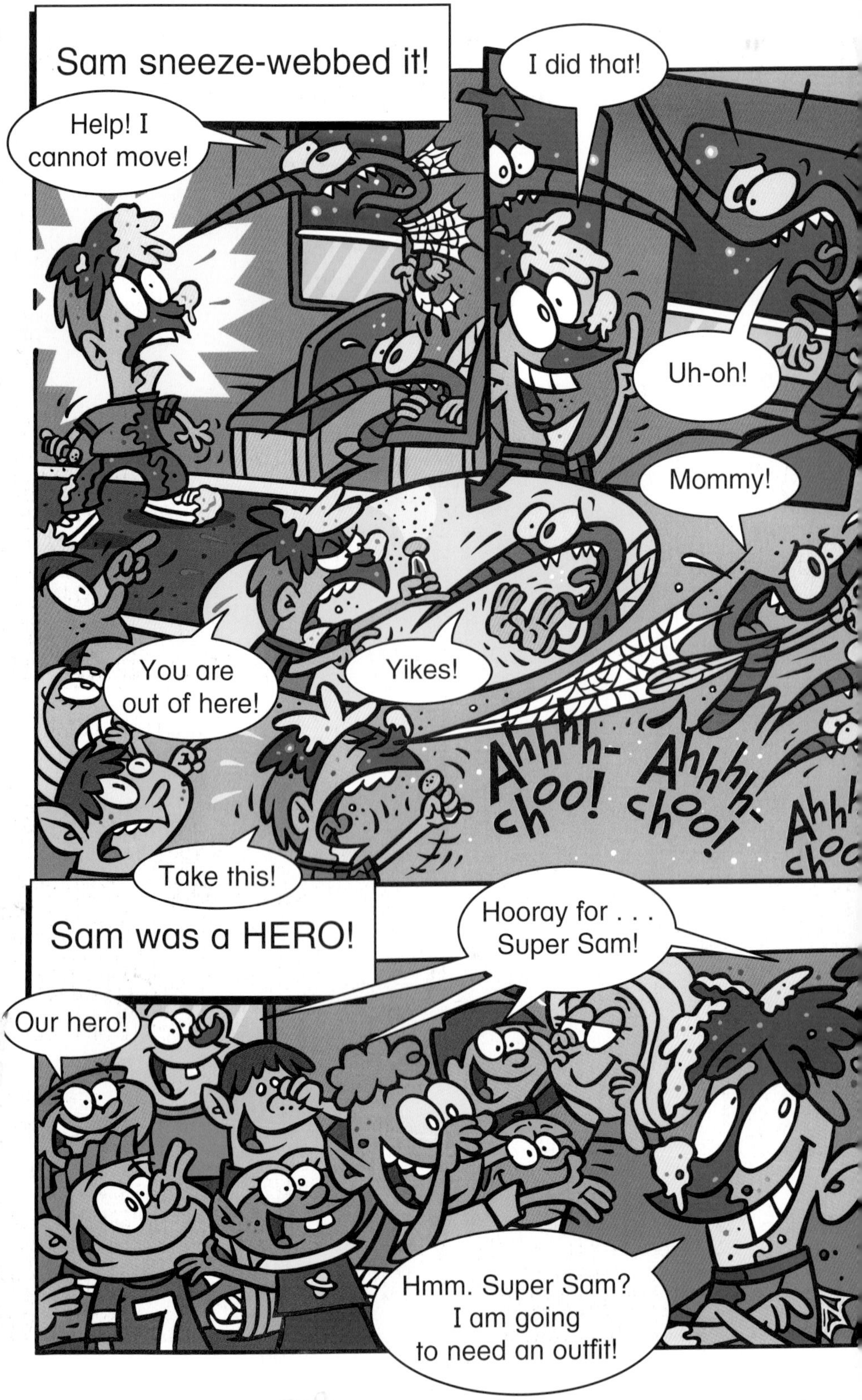
Sam sneeze-webbed it!
Help! I cannot move!
I did that!
Uh-oh!
Mommy!
You are out of here!
Yikes!
Ahhhh-choo! Ahhhh-choo!
Ahh choo
Take this!
Sam was a HERO!
Hooray for . . . Super Sam!
Our hero!
Hmm. Super Sam? I am going to need an outfit!

SAM . . . SUPER SPY?

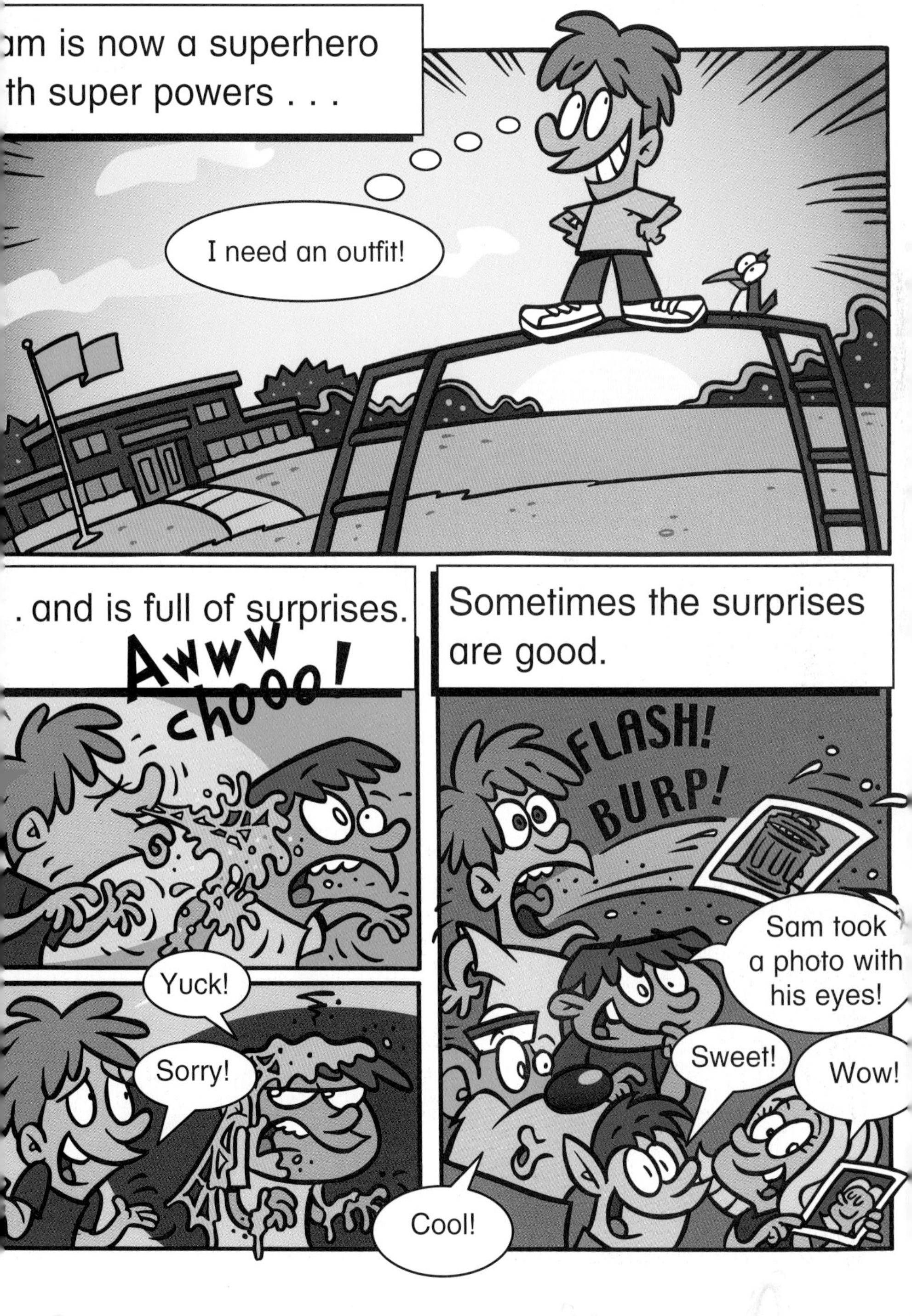
am is now a superhero
th super powers . . .
I need an outfit!
. and is full of surprises.
Awww chooo!
Yuck!
Sorry!
Sometimes the surprises are good.
FLASH!
BURP!
Sam took a photo with his eyes!
Sweet!
Wow!
Cool!

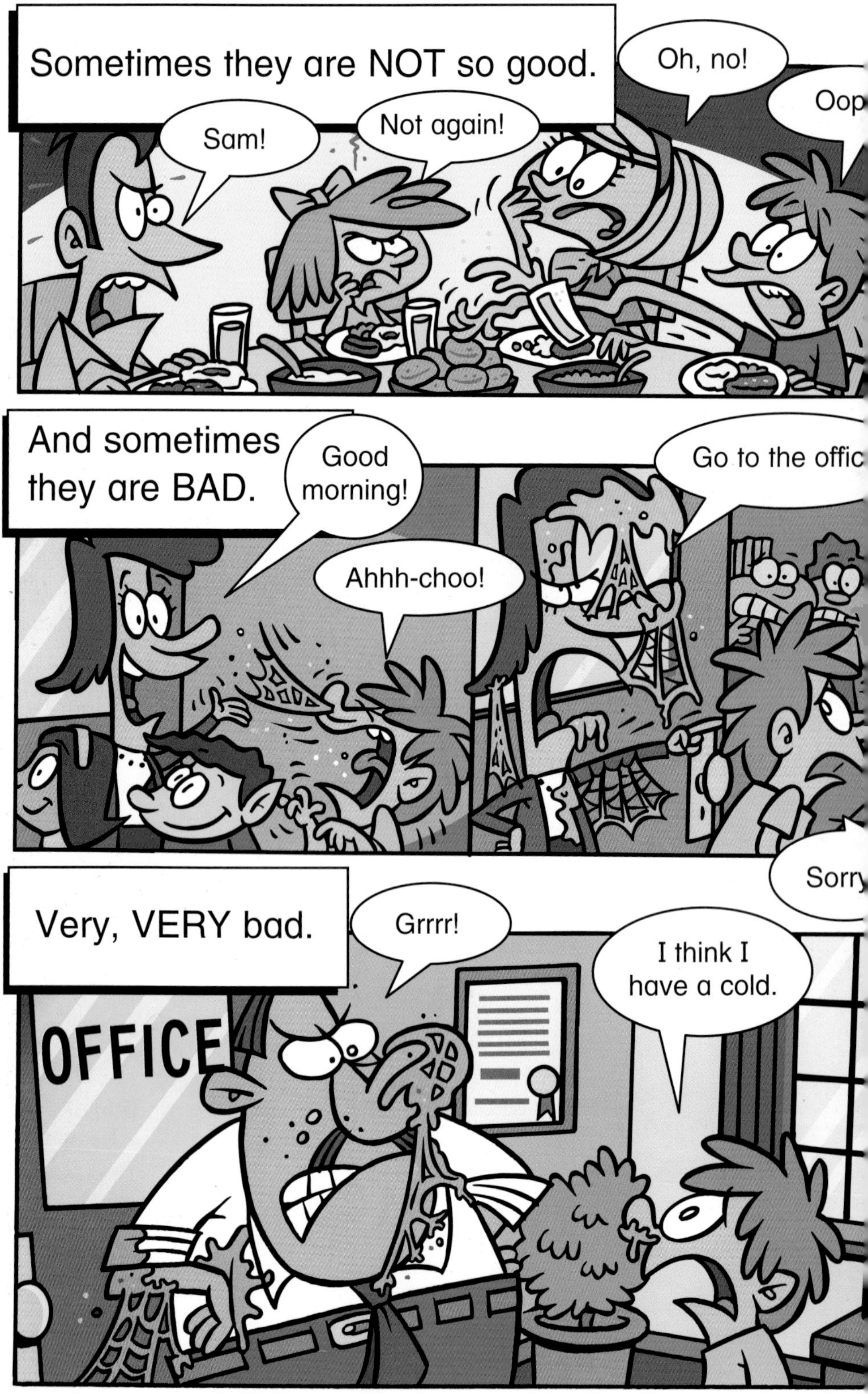
Sometimes they are NOT so good.
Sam!
Not again!
Oh, no!
Oop
And sometimes they are BAD.
Good morning!
Ahhh-choo!
Go to the offic
Sorr
Very, VERY bad.
Grrrr!
OFFICE
I think I have a cold.

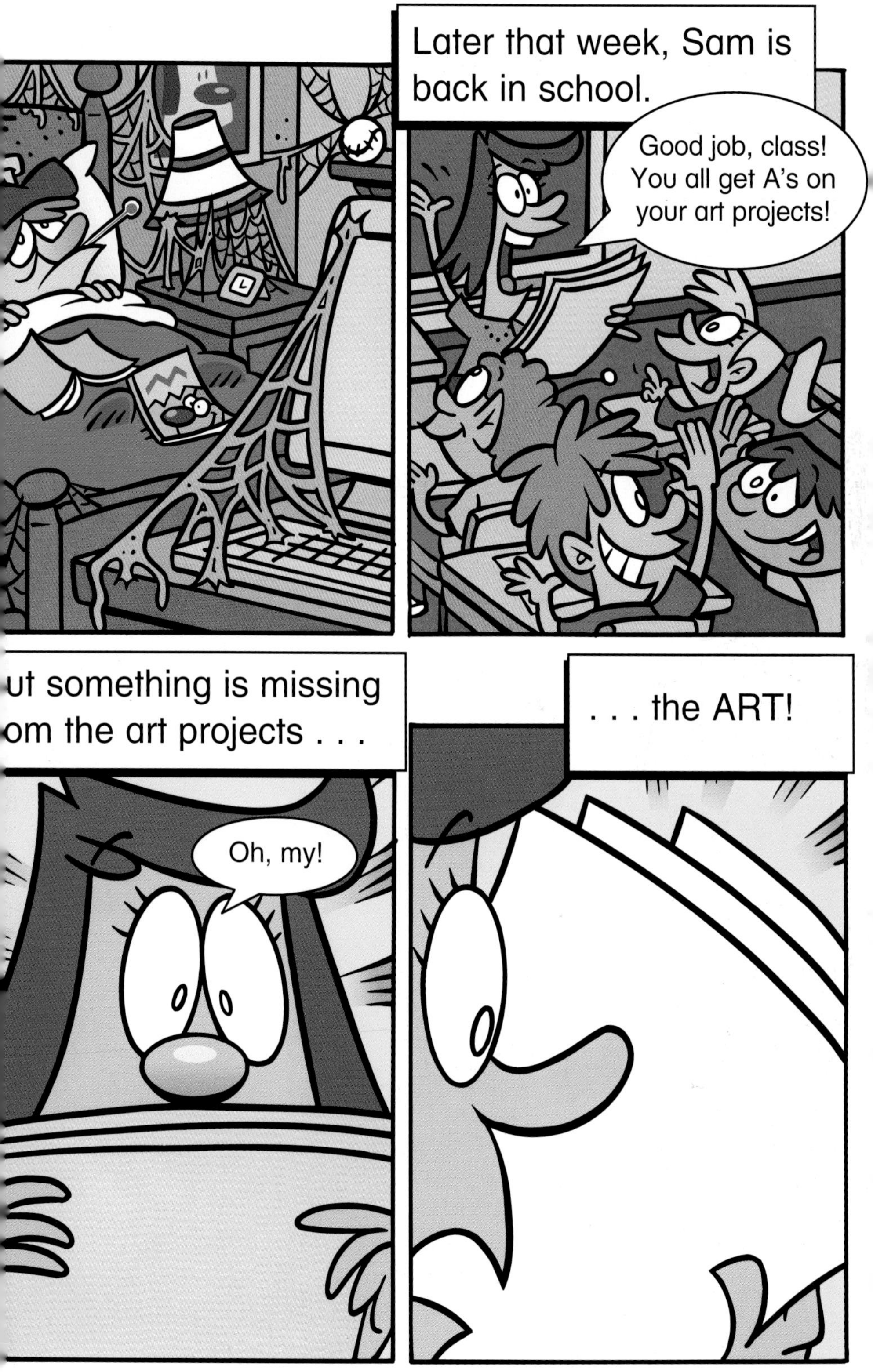
Later that week, Sam is back in school.
Good job, class! You all get A's on your art projects!
ut something is missing om the art projects . . .
. . . the ART!
Oh, my!

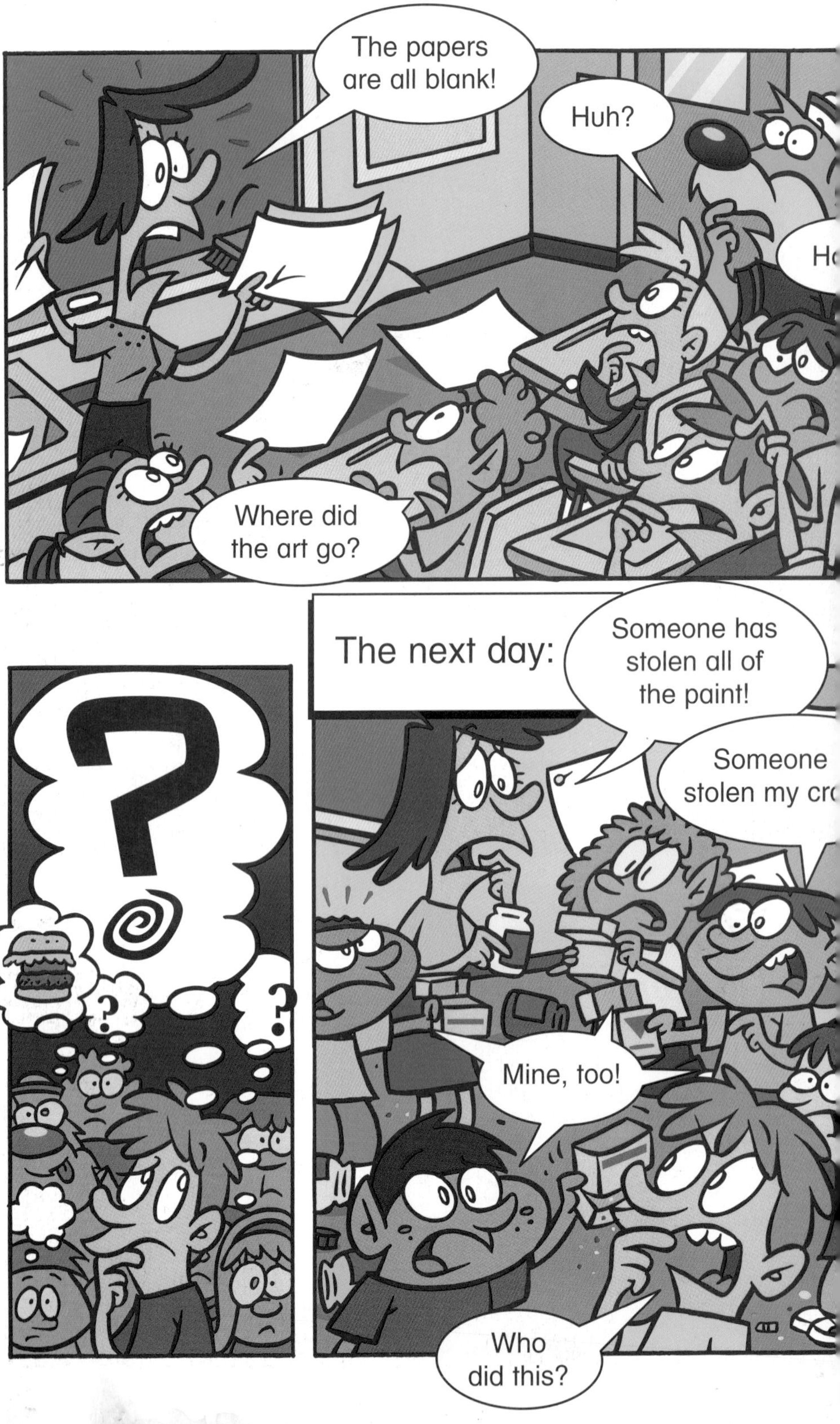
The papers are all blank!
Huh?
Where did the art go?
The next day:
Someone has stolen all of the paint!
Someone
stolen my
Mine, too!
Who did this?

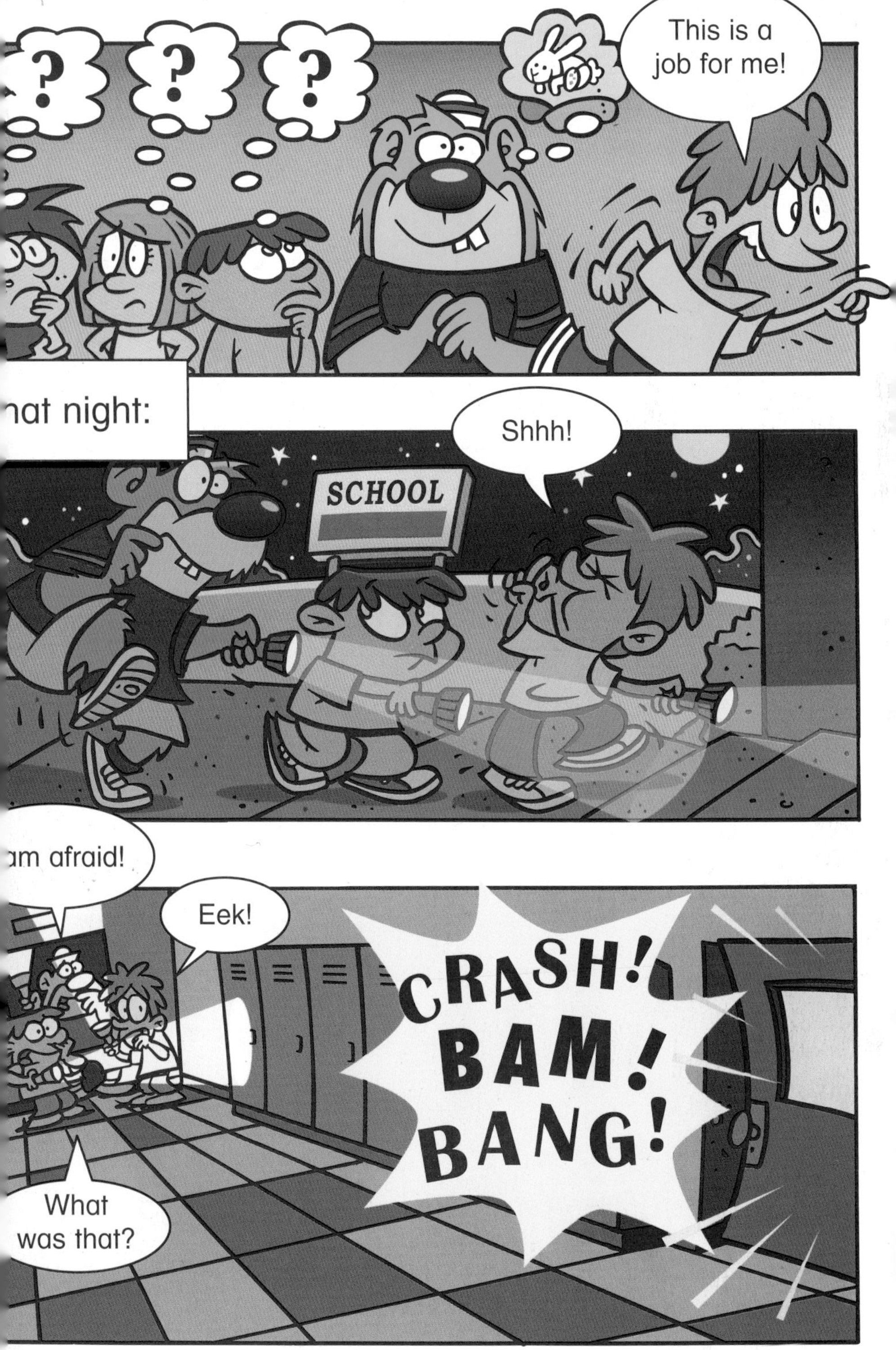
?
?
?
This is a job for me!
ıat night:
Shhh!
SCHOOL
ım afraid!
Eek!
What was that?
CRASH!
BAM!
BANG!

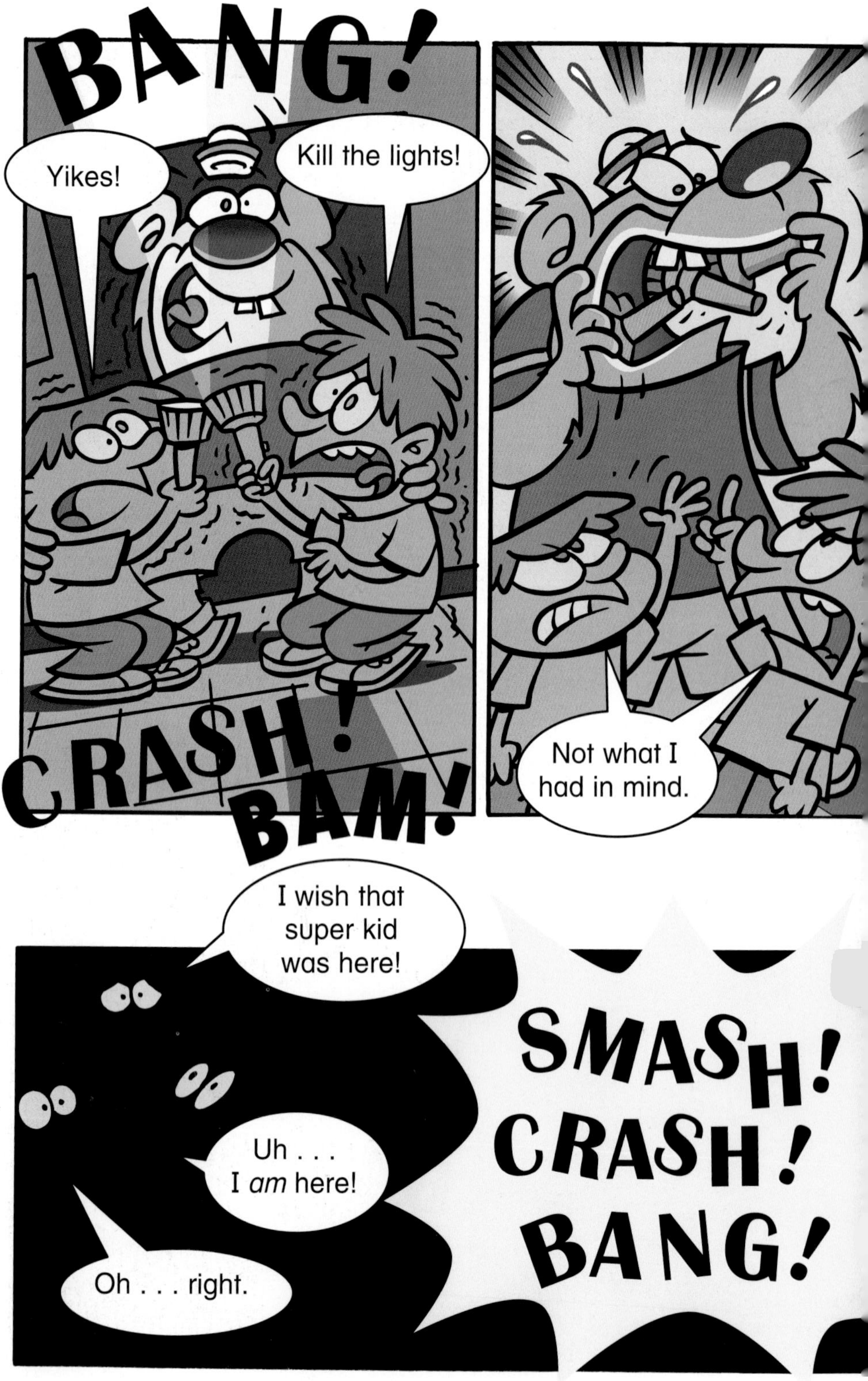
BANG!
Yikes!
Kill the lights!
CRASH!
BAM!
Not what I had in mind.
I wish that super kid was here!
Uh . . . I *am* here!
Oh . . . right.
SMASH!
CRASH!
BANG!

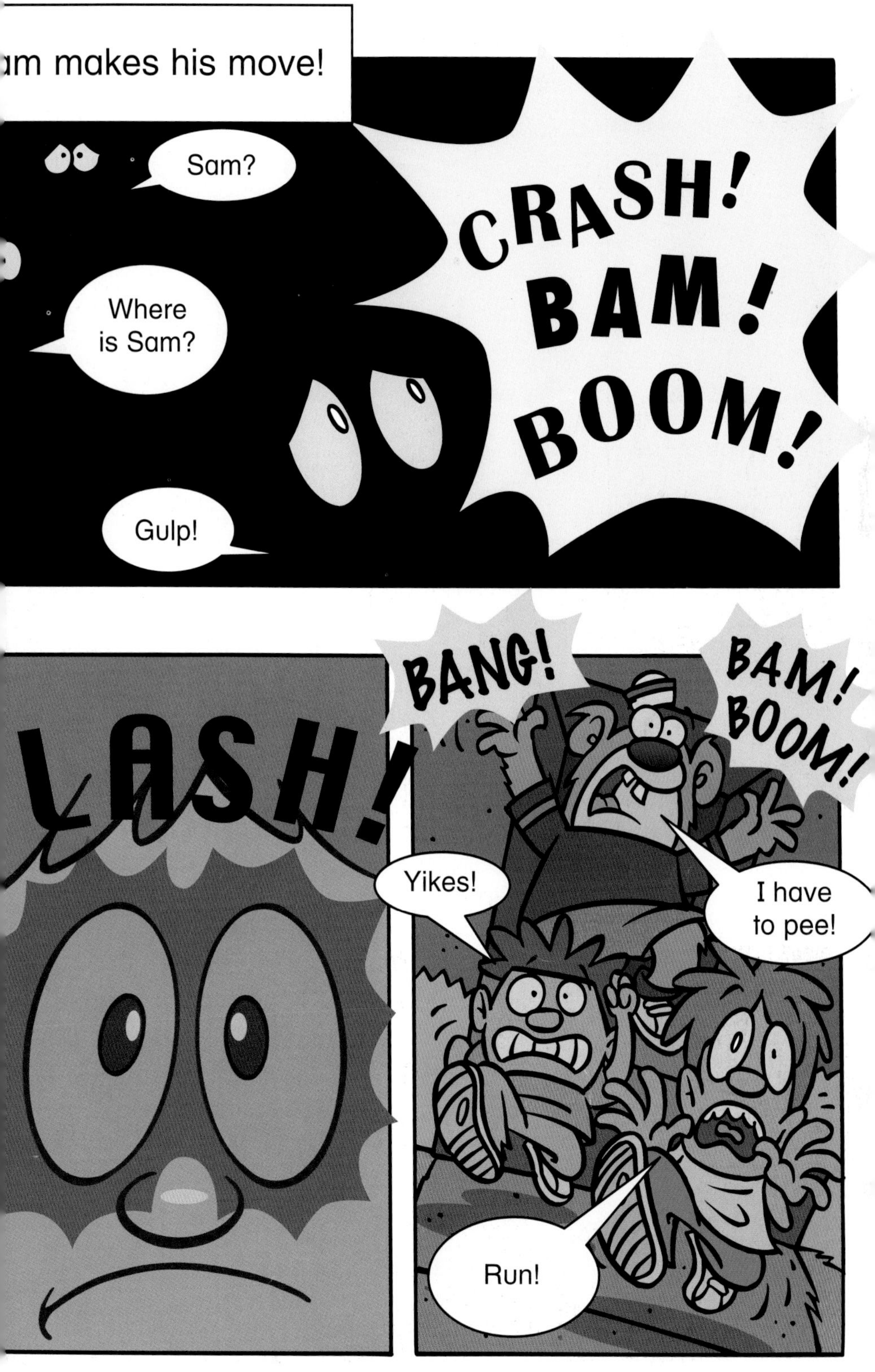

am makes his move!
Sam?
Where is Sam?
Gulp!
CRASH! BAM! BOOM!
LASH!
BANG!
BAM! BOOM!
Yikes!
I have to pee!
Run!

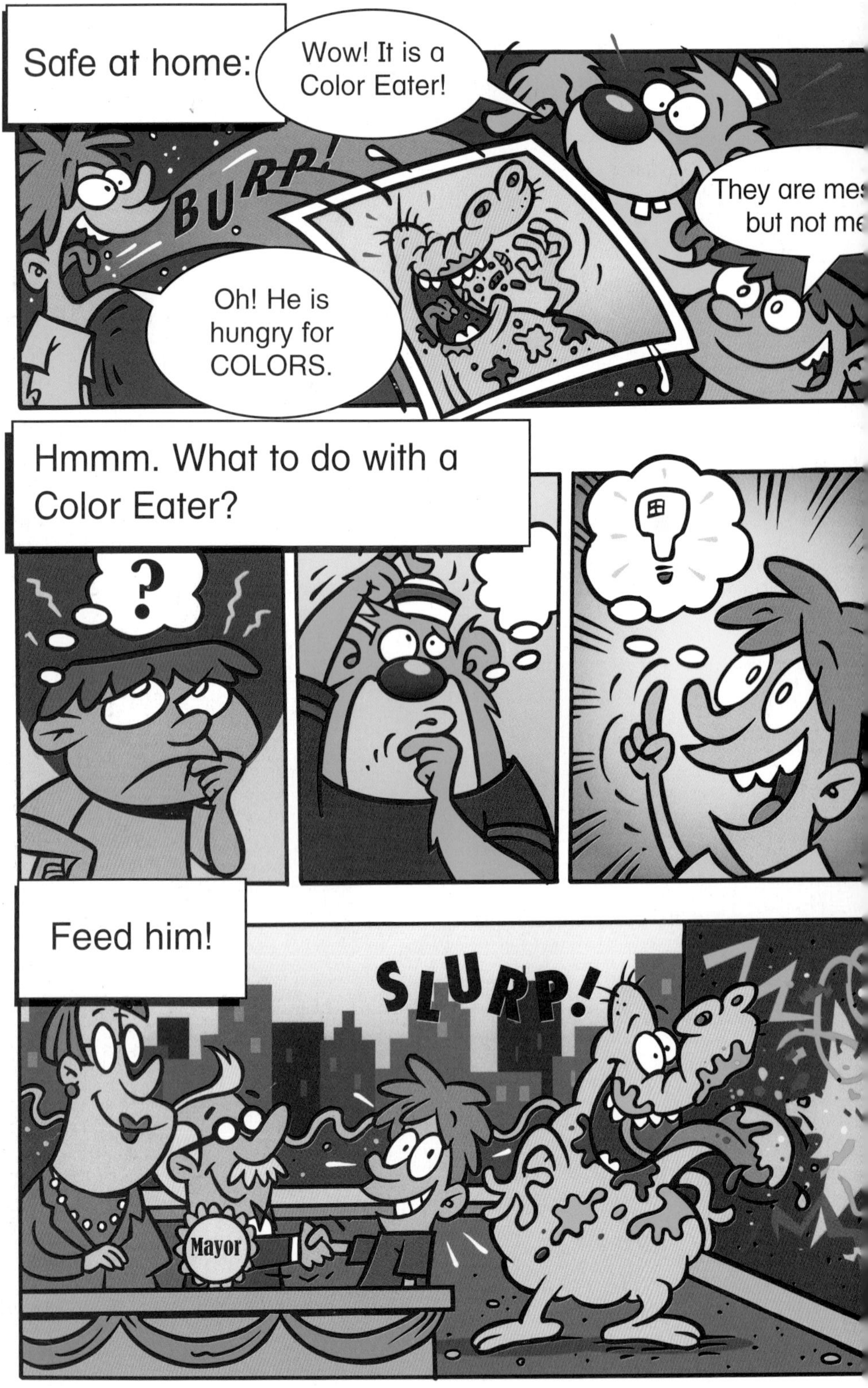
Safe at home:
Wow! It is a Color Eater!
BURP!
Oh! He is hungry for COLORS.
They are
but not
Hmmm. What to do with a Color Eater?
?
Feed him!
SLURP!
Mayor

NOT SAM . . . SUPER SAM!

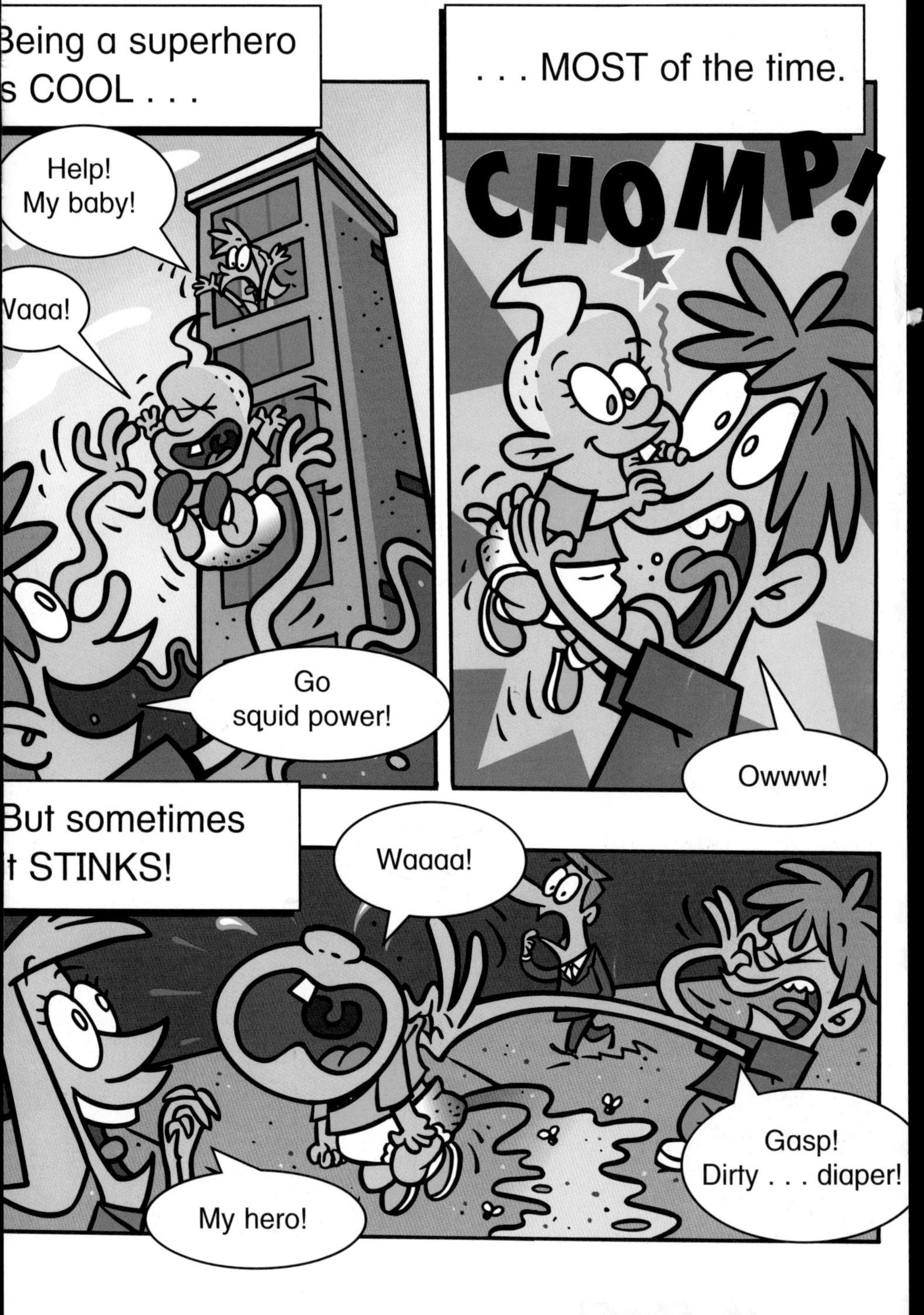
Being a superhero
s COOL . . .
Help!
My baby!
Waaa!
Go
squid power!
. . . MOST of the time.
CHOMP!
Owww!
But sometimes
t STINKS!
Waaaa!
My hero!
Gasp!
Dirty . . . diaper!

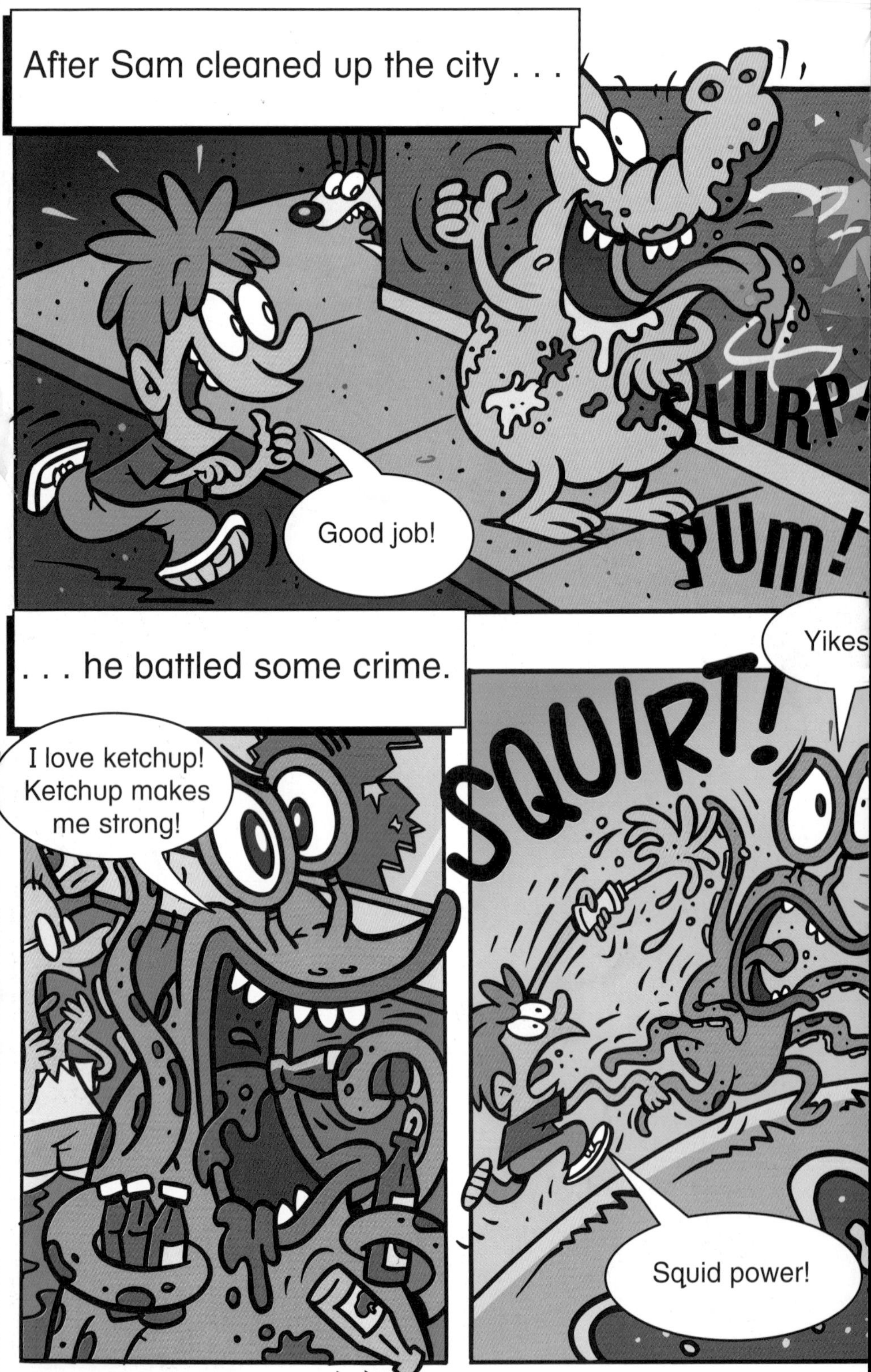
After Sam cleaned up the city . . .
Good job!
SLURP
YUM!
. . . he battled some crime.
I love ketchup! Ketchup makes me strong!
SQUIRT!
Yikes
Squid power!

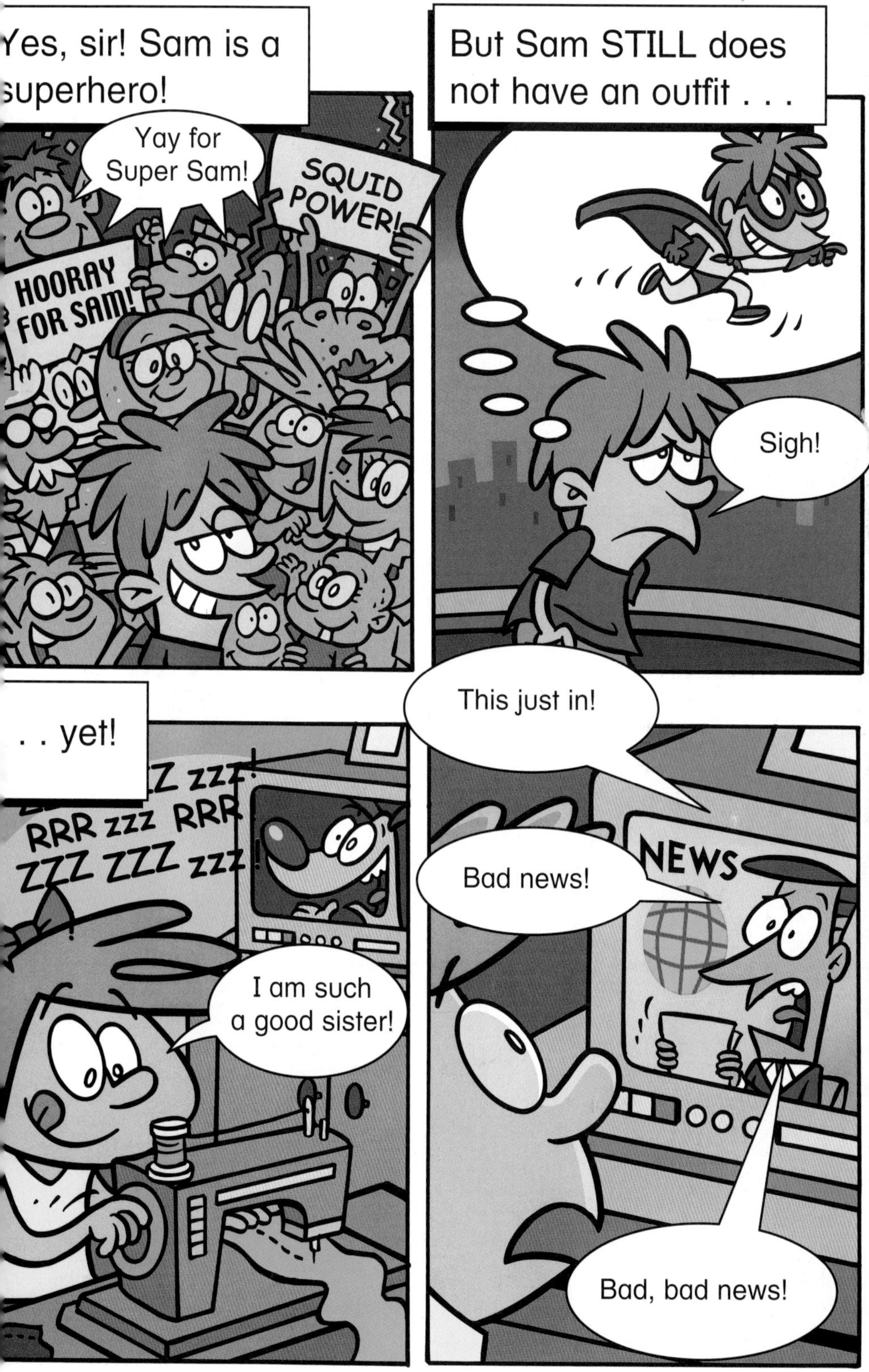
Yes, sir! Sam is a superhero!
Yay for Super Sam!
SQUID POWER!
HOORAY FOR SAM!
But Sam STILL does not have an outfit . . .
Sigh!
. . yet!
RRR zzz RRR
ZZZ ZZZ zzz
I am such a good sister!
This just in!
NEWS
Bad news!
Bad, bad news!

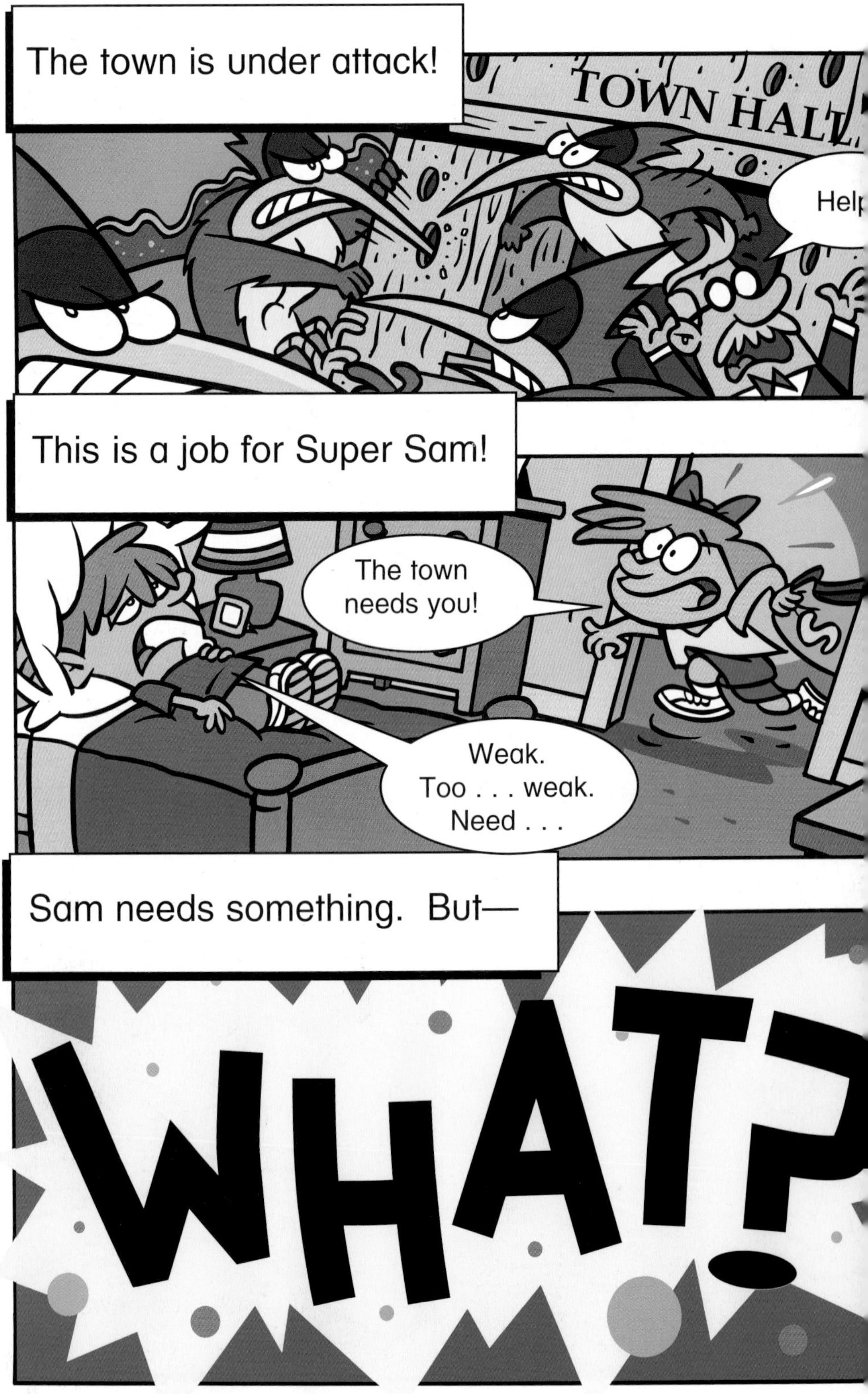
The town is under attack!
TOWN HALL
Help
This is a job for Super Sam!
The town needs you!
Weak. Too . . . weak. Need . . .
Sam needs something. But—
WHAT?

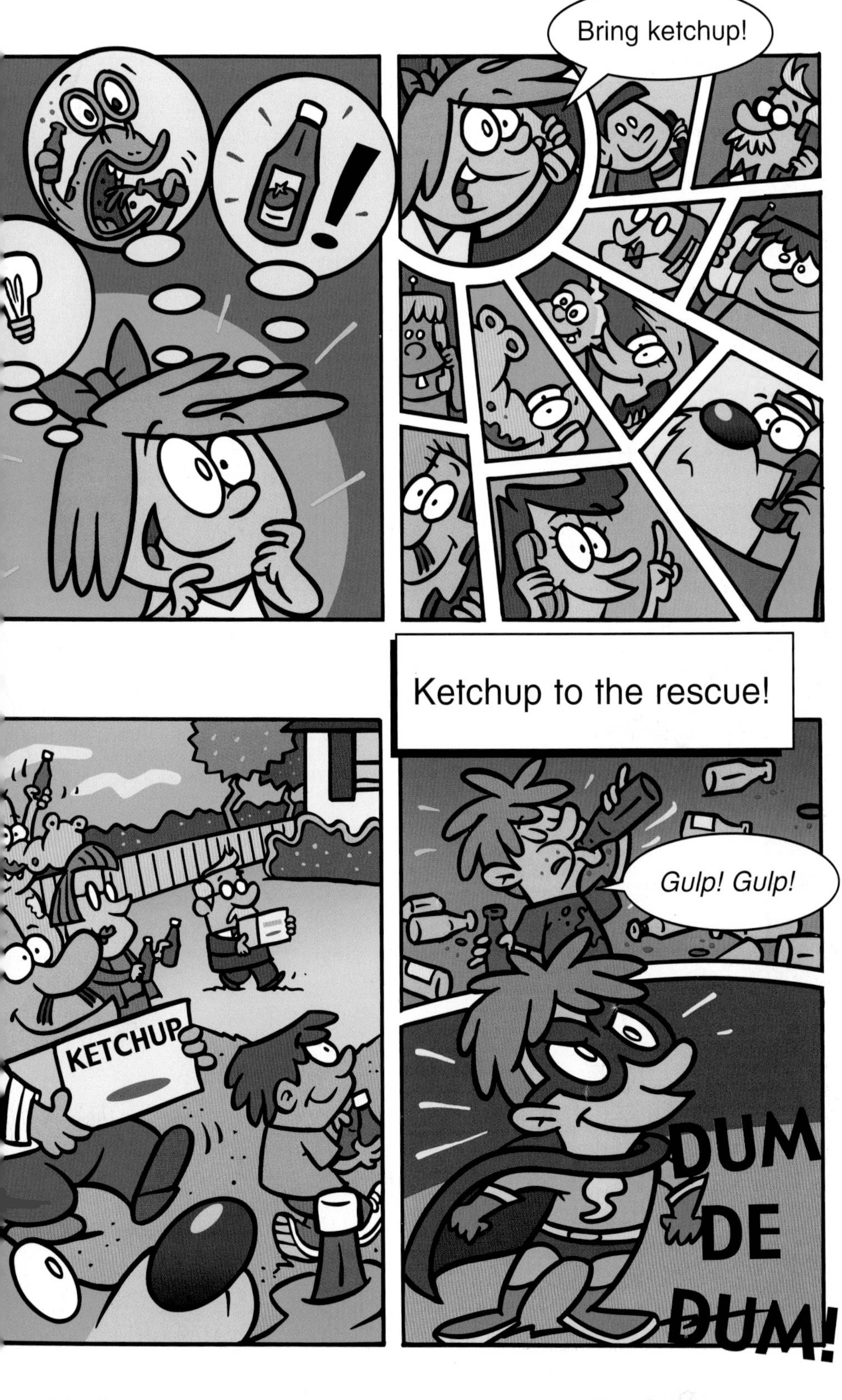
Bring ketchup!
Ketchup to the rescue!
KETCHUP
Gulp! Gulp!
DUM DE DUM!

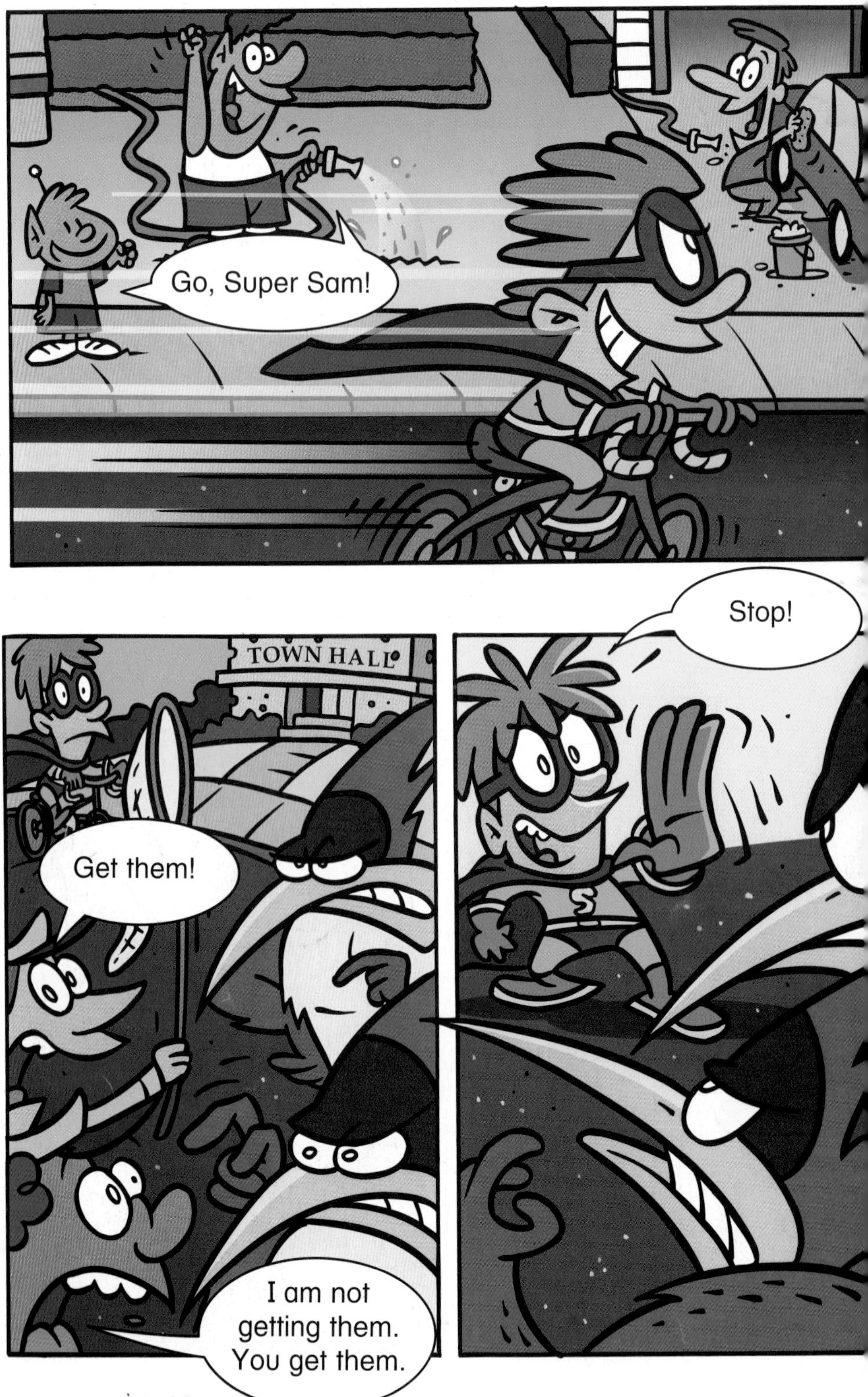
Go, Super Sam!
TOWN HALL
Get them!
I am not getting them. You get them.
Stop!

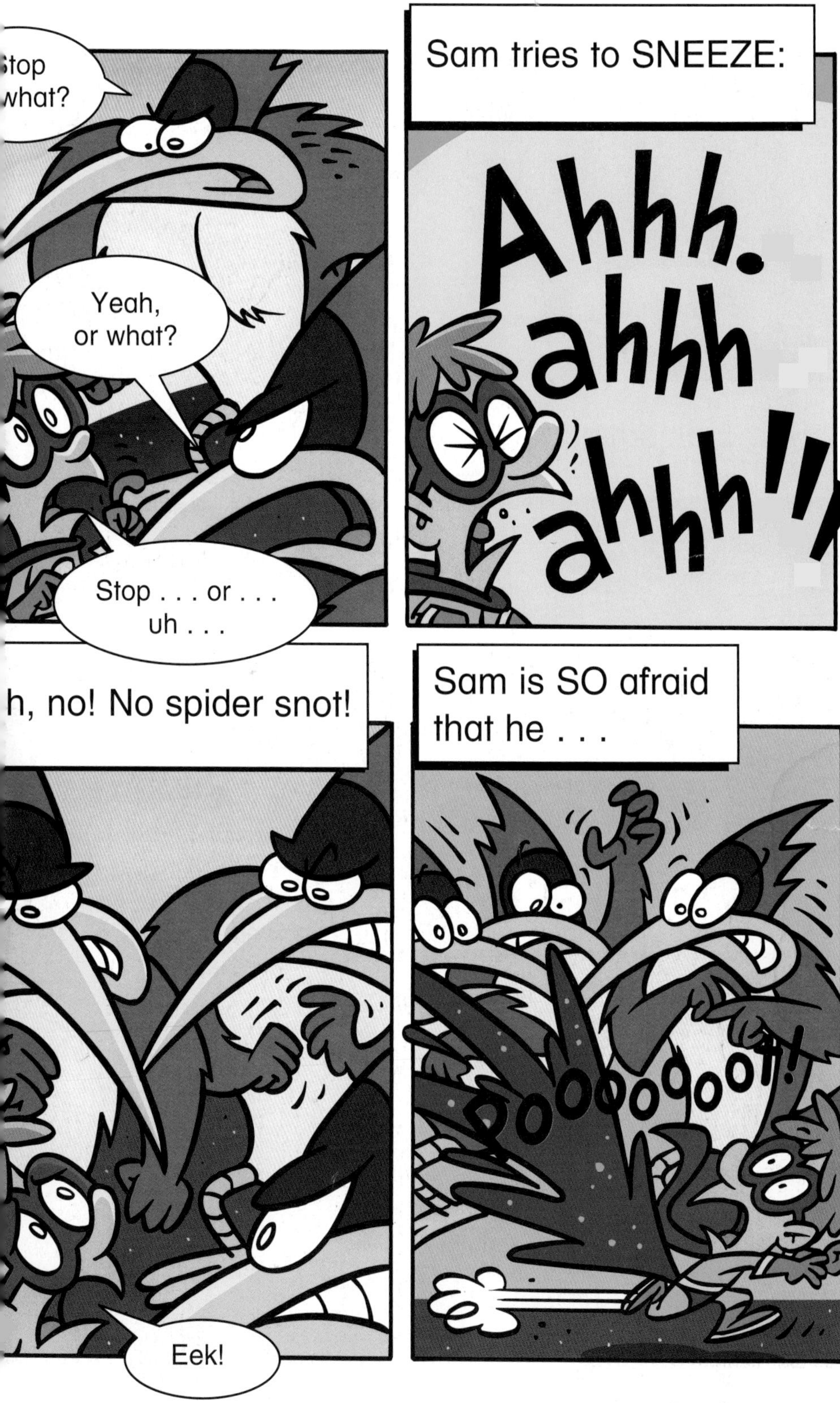

Stop or what?
Yeah, or what?
Stop . . . or . . . uh . . .
Sam tries to SNEEZE:
Ahhh. ahhh ahhh!!!
h, no! No spider snot!
Eek!
Sam is SO afraid that he . . .
Pooooooooff!

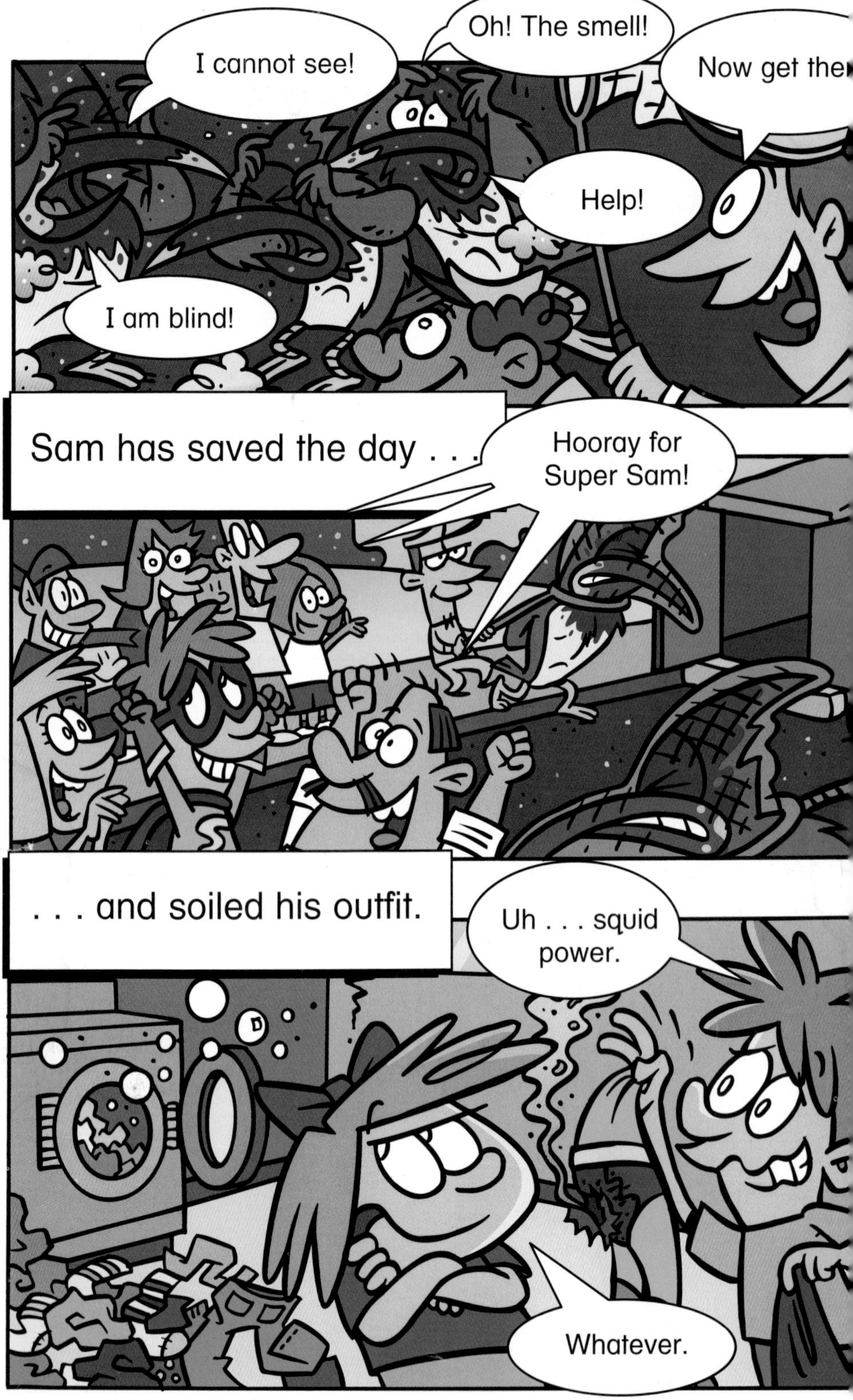
I cannot see!
Oh! The smell!
Now get the
Help!
I am blind!
Sam has saved the day . . .
Hooray for Super Sam!
. . . and soiled his outfit.
Uh . . . squid power.
Whatever.